Let's Go Camping

And
Discover Our Nature

by Miriam Yerushalmi
illustrated by Esther Ido Perez

LET'S GO CAMPING *is a guidebook on how to reach one's full potential.*
It offers guidelines on how to understand and love oneself.
This knowledge enables our precious children to open their minds and hearts
to serve Hashem with joy.

Special thanks to Yaffa Gottlieb,
Chana Leah Schapiro, and Rivkah Vogel for their friendship and incredible help.

Thanks to Chana Motchkin for the poem on the last page
and Yaffa Gottlieb for her poem.

> *A wonderful story and a good read for young reading children and even parents who find life bewildering and often overwhelming.*
>
> •
>
> *Highly recommended for children and adults alike.*
>
> •
>
> *Can change your life and the way you view yourself and others, bringing harmony and family unity.*
>
> *- Rabbi Goldstein*

Let's Go Camping — And Discover Our Nature

First Edition - Adar 5767 / March 2007

ISBN: 0-911643-38-9

Writer's Press Brooklyn, New York
A division of **Aura Printing** 88 Parkville Ave., Brooklyn, NY 11230 718-435-9103

GLOSSARY
Yetzer HaRa – the thoughts in ones heart that tries to trick us not to do good deeds.
Yetzer Tov – the thoughts in one's mind that encourage us to do good deeds.

Printed in China

Gearing Up

Chanale and Chezi were busy packing their backpacks. Soon they would be leaving home to go camping in the mountains with their Abba and Ima.

"I can't wait to get to the top of the highest mountain!" said Chezi. "The higher up you go, the farther you can see! I want to be the very first to reach the top!"

Chanale exclaimed in anticipation, "What an awesome trip it will be! We'll be out in the fresh air, surrounded by flowers, pine trees and waterfalls. How far away are the mountains, Ima?"

"Quite a distance, Chanale," Ima answered. "It will take many hours to get there, but even along the way we'll have fun. You'll be surprised how much we can discover about ourselves by seeing the natural beauty of the world Hashem created."

"Ima, aren't we supposed to live with the times?" asked Chezi. "In this week's Torah portion we read about the Jewish people's travels from place to place before reaching *Eretz Yisrael*. And now we are going on a journey!"

Ima nodded. "That's right, Chezi. Nothing that happens in the world is coincidental."

Ima packed in the new books she had bought to read to the children along the way, and reminded them to take a *siddur*.

"Is everyone ready?" asked Abba.

"Yes!" they answered in unison.

"Then let's go," said Chezi. "I want to be first in the van!"

On the Road

"Why does Chezi always have to be first?" asked Chanale as they all scrambled in and buckled their seatbelts. A moment later Abba was rolling down the driveway.

"Because I like being first," said Chezi. "I'm a first type of person."

"That's true," Abba smiled. "What kind of a person do you think you are, Chanale?"

"Well, I like talking and sharing my ideas. I also like singing!" Chanale answered.

Ima smiled. "Yes, you do like words very much."

"What type of person are you, Ima?" asked Chanale.

"I like to make people happy," she answered.

"And what about you, Abba?" asked Chezi.

"I like learning and thinking deeply about Torah," said Abba.

"So what is the best type of person?" asked Chezi. "Being first, like me, or talking and sharing ideas, like Chanale, or helping others, like Ima, or thinking deeply, like Abba?"

Abba smiled. "They're all good, Chezi. Just as the world is made up of four elements - fire, water, air and earth - so too does every person have parts of the four elements in his personality."

"Really?" Chezi and Chanale asked in surprise.

"Really," Abba explained. "You, Chezi, are fiery by nature. Like a flame of fire you always strive upward, toward the top. Chanale likes words, which are made of air. Chanale uses words to express herself and to say nice things. Ima takes pleasure in helping others, which comes from the element of water that makes things grow. And I like to think, which comes from the element of earth."

"But I do all of those things!" protested Chezi. "I also like to think, help other people and talk!"

Abba nodded his head. "You're right, Chezi. Everyone has all four qualities. But most people have a little more of one than the others."

"I want to have the most of all of them!" exclaimed Chezi.

Excitement Along the Way

Chanale looked out the window and started to sing. Ima gave the children a snack of fruit and apple juice and reminded them to make the right *brachos*. When they were out of the city they said *Tefilas Haderech*, the special prayer asking Hashem for a safe trip.

Everyone was enjoying the scenery. Along the way they saw vegetable gardens and apple orchards. They passed beautiful farms and fields of grain that waved in the breeze. Everything seemed to be growing so nicely. "Take a look around," Abba said. "All of the elements are perfectly balanced. Can you tell me what they are and how they work together?"

"Plants and vegetables grow from the earth," said Chezi. "They get a lot of fresh air from the breeze."

"Plants also need sunshine," said Chanale. "That would be fire, wouldn't it? And the rain waters them."

"That's right!" Ima responded. "And look how green and beautiful the countryside is," she said as she gazed lovingly at her children. *Boruch Hashem*, they also seemed to be growing nicely. Ima hoped this camping trip would be a "growing" experience for the whole family.

Stories Come to Life

As Abba was looking at the map to find their way, Ima took out one of the new books she had brought along and asked, "Who would like to hear some stories from *The Tales of Tzadikim*?"

"We do!" they answered.

Ima began to read as their Abba continued driving toward their destination. The hours passed quickly. The children sat mesmerized, enjoying every detail.

Chezi said, "It's really amazing how our *tzadikim* cared so much about every single Jew.

Chanale piped in, "And they weren't even scared to be alone when they spent hours in the fields praying and learning Torah. I remember learning how Avraham, Yitzchak and Yaakov became closer to Hashem when they saw the beauty of the world around them. They spent many hours outdoors, thinking about Hashem."

"So did Dovid Hamelech," added Chezi thoughtfully. "He played beautiful music on his harp and wrote Tehillim while taking care of his sheep in the meadows."

"There are great *tzadikim* in every generation who follow in their footsteps," said Abba.

Welcome to the Mountains

The scenery continued to change as they approached the campground. Houses became few and far between and soon they were surrounded by tall pines. Abba turned off the highway and onto a narrow winding road. Up and up the mountains they went, higher and higher! Down below, they could see tree tops. A few minutes later Abba turned off the road and drove slowly over a gravel path. Facing them was a big sign:

"WELCOME TO THE ADIRONDACKS."

"There isn't any snow!" exclaimed Chezi. "I thought there was supposed to be snow up here? I wanted to make a big snowball and throw it off the top!"

"Oh, but it is so beautiful even without the snow!" said Chanale.

The children jumped out and stood for a few minutes taking in the splendor of the wilderness. It was a breathtaking sight. But even with all the excitement, Chanale and Chezi remembered to help unload the camping gear and supplies from the van.

"Who's ready for a real adventure?" Abba asked, putting on his backpack.

"We are, Abba!" replied Chezi. "We've been waiting for this all year!"

"Then let's go!" he exclaimed, leading the way.

As they set out Ima announced, "Now we will have a chance to get closer to Hashem, the way our Avos did."

Roots and Trees

The family started walking along the trail. They hadn't gone far, however, when they had to stop. A huge tree had fallen down and was blocking their path.

"What are we going to do?" asked Chanale "I don't want to have to turn back."

"Don't worry, Chanale. We can just climb over where the tree trunk is split."

The children followed Abba. "Look here," Abba said, sounding like a tour guide.

"Do you see the rings in the tree trunk? Every ring shows the tree's growth for an entire year."

Chanale suddenly had a thought. "Abba! There are so many rings in this tree. It must be very old. Could this be the *Eitz Hachaim* from Gan Eden?"

"You never know," Abba said with a wink.

"You are so cute!" Chezi exclaimed as he hugged his younger sister.

"Abba, look how thick these roots are," noted Chezi. "I learned that the closer the roots are to the trunk, the more important they are for the tree's health and vitality."

"That is very true," said Abba.

Ima smiled. "The Torah states that man is like a tree in the field. When our own thoughts, speech and actions are connected to the Torah, they give us strength just like the closer roots of the tree give the tree its strength." she explained.

"Ima, there are so many things we can learn about ourselves from nature, even from roots and trees," said Chezi.

Abba glanced at his watch. "Well, we'd better be on our way if we plan on pitching our tents before dark."

A Lesson in Everything

The shadows grew longer as the family continued along the trail toward the campsite. Passing a field of orange lilies, they stopped to rest and admire the flowers.

Chanale bent down and took a sniff. "This flower smells like perfume. And this one smells like candy. There are so many different sweet smelling flowers!"

"Each flower is special in its own way, just like people," said Ima. "In the same way that each blossom is one-of-a-kind, every person has their own unique talents. So let us all blossom like a beautiful flower," Ima said with a cute smile.

"Oh, Ima," Chezi answered, "I'd rather be a tree. They're stronger."

"I'd rather be a flower!" countered Chanale. "Besides, flowers are strong in their own way. If a big wind comes along and blows a big, stiff tree can fall down, but flowers bend in the breeze and don't break."

"You see, children," Ima explained, "There is something to learn from everything that G-d created."

"That's one of the reasons G-d made them," Abba added.

"A flower's fragrance fades away," said Ima, "but our mitzvos and good deeds last forever. That reminds me of a poem my dear friend Michal Ahava once wrote to me. Would you like to hear it?"

The children listened as she recited:

Ever-friend
If you were a tree, you would surely be an evergreen
Spreading your brightness and warmth even in winter
With your bright smile and warm hugs, you're always there
On you, the sun never ceases to shine
Never withering,
You are beautiful always.
Thank you for being my sunshine,
I am happy, for you are an ever-friend of mine.

"You, my dear children are my sunshine," Ima said with a sparkle in her eye.

"I want to be your ever-friend, Ima," Chanale said smiling.

"Me too!" Chezi joined in.

"We will always be ever-friends," Ima said, giving them a hug.

Water, Water Everywhere - Even in a Stick

As the family made headway up the trail a spectacular sight greeted them. A gigantic waterfall came into view, tumbling down the side of the mountain and roaring into a small lake. Everyone stopped to admire the scenery. Ima decided it was the perfect spot to take a break and enjoy a snack of corn chips and fresh spring water.

"This waterfall," Ima remarked, "reminds me of what we were talking about before. Do you remember that Abba told you that everything in the world is made up of four elements, and that water is one of them?"

"Yes," said Chezi, "but how can that be?"

To answer Chezi, Abba bent down and picked up a stick from the ground. "Do you see this piece of wood?" he asked holding it up. "Believe it or not, even this dried-out stick contains the element of water, although you can't see it. Later, when we build our campfire with this stick, all that will remain of the stick is ashes, while the water inside will be released.

"Oh, I get it!" Chezi caught on. "The smoke shows that the water is being released from the stick."

"You got it!" Abba said with a smile "As we said before, every person is also made up of these four elements, which can be used for either good or bad. The same element that helps us develop our special character traits also, *chas veshalom*, can be used negatively. Let me give you an example:

A person whose element of water is dominant likes to acquire things. No matter how many things he has, it's never enough for him. In other words, he is never satisfied with what he already has."

"This doesn't mean," Abba continued, "that a person who is born like that is stuck. He can learn to channel his natural inclination into something positive. Instead of wanting more things, he can transform his desire into wanting to do more mitzvos and learn more Torah."

"Can you think of any other specific examples?" asked Ima.

"Well," Chezi said slowly, "the water element might make him want to daven longer or say more Tehillim."

"Or give more and more *tzedakah*," Chanale added.

"Those are very good examples," said Abba. He swayed his hand around to indicate the delightful scenery. "We see in nature that water is necessary for life. People need water when they are thirsty. Plants and animals need water to survive. Rain is a wonderful blessing from Hashem that makes things grow and sustains life here on Earth.

"But too much water is a bad thing," said Chezi, shaking his head knowingly. "Flooding can cause lots and lots of damage. I guess what you're saying is that the element of water - and all the other elements - needs to be balanced and used in the right way."

"That's right," Ima responded.

The Puff and the Element of Air

As they walked, Chanale began chatting to Chezi about an unpleasant incident that happened in school. Ima thought it was the perfect time to talk more about the element of air.

"Look up at the sky, children," Ima said. "See how beautiful it is. The air is clear and the breeze is refreshing. Not only do we use air for breathing, but as you know whenever we speak air comes out of our mouths.

"Now, I want both of you to try this: Put your hands in front of your mouth and blow. Feel the air coming out? Now stop blowing. This is something you can control. You can blow or not blow, just as you can choose to speak or not to speak."

Chezi and Chanale giggled as they blew on their hands and emitted little puffs.

"You can't see it with your eyes," Ima continued, "but our Rabbis tell us that what we say has a very big effect on the air. When we say holy words, the air around us becomes pure. Can you think of other ways you can use the element of air for good?" she asked.

"I know," Chanale answered in excitement. "You can say *brachos*."

Chezi added, "You can speak to someone and cheer them up when they're sad, or you can give someone advice when they need help."

"Those are great ideas!" Ima exclaimed. "You know, we really have to be careful about what comes out of our mouths. Do you know what it says in the Gemara? A happy man is one who knows what to say and when to say it."

At that moment they happened to pass an old campsite and noticed ashes and partially-burned logs of wood. "Hey, this reminds me of something we read in *The Little Midrash Says*," Chanale piped up. "Remember the two Yiddin who were traveling in the desert and started a camp fire with *rosem*-wood to cook their food?"

"Yeah," her brother replied. "A year later they came to the same place and stepped on the ashes in their bare feet, the embers were still hot inside!"

"The Midrash explains that *lashon hara* is compared to *rosem*-wood because when someone hears something bad about another person, he may seem to forget about it, but deep inside it keeps on glowing. Unfortunately, the negative effect of *lashon hara* lasts for a long time."

Setting Up Camp

The children were getting a little tired. "I am very proud of both of you for holding up for so long," Abba said. "If you want, we can take another break."

"Nah, let's move on," Chezi answered determinedly. They kept walking and finally arrived at the campsite. It was an amazing sight. Perched atop a hill, they could see the surrounding countryside for miles in every direction.

"What a perfect place this is - well worth the hike!" Chanale exclaimed. "It makes me want to sing!" So she did:

> *A lovely lake and waterfall*
> *This campsite really has it all.*
> *Here I want to stay, it is so pretty.*
> *Who wants to go back to the city?*

Everyone laughed. Then it was Ima's turn to recite:

> *A lovely lake and waterfall*
> *G-d has really given us all.*
> *It's wonderful here, where we are higher*
> *But for cooking, we need a fire.*

Not to be outdone, Abba added:

> *This lovely lake and waterfall*
> *Soon sun will set behind it all.*
> *Let's set up tent in this lovely park.*
> *Let's do it now, before it's dark.*

Finally Chezi sang out:

> *I'd help, but really I'm imploring.*
> *I'd so much rather go exploring.*
> *To climb this mountain and not to stop*
> *Until I reach the very top!*

Everyone laughed and got to work. Abba found a flat spot to pitch the tent and started clearing away the rocks. At first Chezi and Chanale helped out enthusiastically, but as the novelty faded and the job became more tedious, they worked more and more slowly. Eventually, they plopped to the ground.

Abba said, "You kids were real troopers today. I am very impressed by how you kept the pace. Seeing you tired though reminds me of the element of earth."

Abba found a stick and formed out the letters E-A-R-T-H in the dirt. "That spells the word 'earth,'" he explained. "The element of earth can make a person feel sad, lazy and tired. Imagine having to always carry around heavy bags of dirt on your back. It would slow you down and tire you out.

"But the element of earth can also be used for good," he continued. "Sometimes, it's a good thing to go slowly. Can you give me an example?"

"That's a tough one," answered Chanale.

"Yeah," agreed her brother.

"Keep thinking, you'll come up with something," Abba said, waiting patiently.

"I know!" Chezi exclaimed. "You can slow down the speed of your davening, so you can say the words more clearly and with greater intent."

"And brachos, too," added Chanale eagerly.

"Right, you get the point," he answered. "The element of earth can also help you slow down to avoid a bad behavior, giving you that extra time to think before you act. Let's say that someone teases a classmate in school. How do you think the classmate might respond?"

Chezi shrugged and made a furrow in the dirt with his toe. "Tease him back, I guess."

Abba continued, "The child whose feelings were hurt might want to lash out and say something mean, but he can also stop himself and consider whether it's the right thing to do."

"I have the perfect story to illustrate this lesson," said Ima.

Think Before You Speak

"It was the night before the first day of school," Ima began, "and a teacher was getting ready for the upcoming day. He organized his clothes and set the alarm clock for an hour early just to make sure he got to school on time.

"The next morning he stood at the bus stop, but to his surprise the bus didn't arrive. He wasn't worried, as the next bus would bring him to school on time, but that bus didn't arrive either. By now it was getting late.

"The teacher decided to hail a taxi, even though it was very expensive. As he got into the car, he reminded himself of his Rosh Hashanah resolution not to speak before stopping to think of the appropriate response.

"He arrived at school just as the first bell was ringing. Rushing through the halls to his classroom, he noticed one of his students pointing to his watch with a smirk on his face. The first thought that came to his mind was 'How dare you! What a disrespectful child to embarrass his teacher!' Nonetheless, he remembered his resolution and did not react.

"Recess came. As he pondered the earlier incident, the same boy ran up to him and again pointed to his watch. 'I've been waiting for this all summer!' the boy said to his teacher excitedly. 'You're my favorite teacher, and I wanted to show you the new watch I got from my Dad for my birthday.'

"As you can imagine, the teacher was shocked. Not only had he entirely misread the boy's behavior, but he had no clue that he was this child's favorite teacher. He thanked Hashem that he did not respond immediately, because had he done so, he would have embarrassed the boy and hurt their relationship."

Ima sighed. "That is why it is important to also know the language of silence. Keeping quiet and thinking before speaking can save you from a lot of trouble.

The Element of Fire

After the children had rested awhile, Abba suggested they start building the campfire. He asked them to find some big rocks so they could make a circle to surround the fire pit. Chezi then helped place some logs in the pit. Soon the campfire was ablaze.

As the fire crackled and popped, Chanale and Chezi started to quarrel. Each one wanted to sit on the biggest rock.

"I want to sit on that one," said Chanale.

"But, I was here first," countered Chezi.

"You two seem upset," Abba broke in. He pointed to the flames. "Take a look at the fire. Fire, like all the elements, has a good and a bad side to it. We use fire to cook our dinner and to keep warm, but fire can also burn and destroy."

"And it isn't good to be arrogant or burning with anger," said Ima.

"What does arrogant mean?" Chanale asked.

"Arrogant," Abba explained, "means acting like a big shot and thinking you are the best, as if you own the whole world. The more arrogant a person is, the more easily he becomes angry. A humble person, by contrast, doesn't become angry or offended so easily. He works on his character and speaks kindly to others, even if they aren't so nice to him. Instead of using the element of fire in a bad way, he uses it to warm his heart and move closer to Hashem and to his fellow Jew.

"Do you know what helps me be more forgiving?" added Ima. "I try to remember that everyone makes mistakes at one time or another. I know that I'm not perfect, so I say to myself, 'why should I expect someone else to be perfect?' This really helps me stay calm and avoid getting upset."

"That is really helpful advice," said Chezi. "But how can you be fiery and humble at the same time?"

"The answer is in the fire," said Abba. "Do you see where the flames have died down, but the embers are still glowing? That's where the hottest part of the fire is. A person with a fiery personality has a choice. He can fan his flames to make himself angry and proud, or he can use his greatest warmth to show love for Hashem and spread excitement for *yiddishkeit*.

"The inside fire is the best," Chezi said. "That's the kind I want to have!"

"Me too!" Chanale agreed.

"Everyone has two inclinations," Abba continued, "a *yetzer hara** that wants us to use these elements for the bad, and a *yetzer tov** that wants us to use them for the good. Our job is to make sure the *yetzer hara* doesn't trick us."

"But how do we fight the *yetzer hara*, Abba?" asked Chanale.

"All of the *mitzvos* we do weaken it," Abba explained. "Hashem doesn't expect us to win this battle overnight."

"Have you ever seen a newborn baby suddenly stand up and start running?" Ima asked.

"No," Chezi giggled. "A little baby can't even crawl yet."

"Exactly," said Ima. "Our own development also comes in stages. Keeping this in mind helps us to be more realistic and patient about our progress. It's a process, but the better we understand ourselves, the more self-confident we become. The most important thing is to always keep trying and never give up. Hashem has given us everything we need in order to reach our best."

"*Bli neder*, Ima, I'm going to try to use my four elements only for the good," said Chanale.

"Same here!" said Chezi.

"Do you know what else?" Ima continued. "The more good you do, the easier it is to turn away from bad."

"So now, every time you see one of the four elements in nature—whenever you take a drink of water or feel a breeze blowing, see a candle burning or notice a plant growing in the soil—let it be a reminder to use your own elements in a positive way. That way everything we encounter in the world is personally meaningful to us."

A Little Light

By now the children were very sleepy. A huge moon had risen in the sky. All around them they could hear the crickets chirping. Soon the hooting of the owls would join the nightly symphony.

Abba glanced at his watch. "It's getting late, children. We're going to need a good night's sleep for tomorrow's hike back. Let's get our flashlights and our sleeping bags."

After they got their flashlights and entered the tent, Chezi exclaimed, "Isn't it neat how such a little flashlight can get rid of so much darkness?"

"You know," said Abba, "light is often used as a mashal, an allegory, for mitzvahs. Each mitzvah has its own special flame that illuminates the world."

"We had such a fun day," Ima said. "We passed through so many different places."

"Just like the Yidden in the desert," added Chanale.

"Do you remember what we learned in this week's Torah portion? The Jewish people went through forty-two different journeys to get to Eretz Yisrael. This is a lesson for us, that we Yidden never like to stay still. In fact, our nature is to go from one mitzvah to another and reach higher and higher levels of holiness. We are all growing and advancing. Our growth isn't a one-stop journey, but a step-by-step process of many journeys.

"This camping trip has made us think about our own journey through life," she said. "Before we go to sleep, let's thank Hashem for this wonderful opportunity." As usual, Ima reminded the children to say Shema.

"Good night, I love you." Ima whispered, giving them a hug and a kiss.

"I love you too," they responded as they kissed and hugged their Ima goodnight.

A New Day

The next morning the children awoke to the sound of birds singing. Abba was already building a new campfire. They sang Modeh Ani and washed negel vasser. As soon as they exited the tent they noticed a mother bird hovering over her baby chicks.

"Ima, Abba - look!" the children called, pointing at the nest. Just then, the mother bird took off and flew high into the sky.

Concerned, Chanale asked, "Ima, where did the mommy bird go? Why did she leave her babies?"

"The mommy bird went to get the baby chicks some food," Ima answered gently. "Don't worry, she's coming back. You know just like the eagle carries its chicks on its wings, so too Hashem always carries B'nei Yisrael his children and protects us."

Just then they saw an eagle soaring majestically in the bright blue sky. It was the perfect conclusion to their wonderful camping trip. Abba, Ima and the children sang in unison:

As the eagle flies
   through the open skies
On its noble wings
   our prayers are soaring
Our destiny is unfolding

Next Year in Yerushalayim Habnuya!